The Little Mermaid
& other fairy tales

**A PICTURESQUE RETELLING
WITH POP-OUT CHARACTERS**

WELBECK

Retold by Lauren Holowaty

Illustrated by Maddy Vian

CONTENTS

The Princess and the Pea

Thumbelina

The Little
Mermaid

Far out at sea and deep in the bottom of
the ocean, the Sea King ruled the underwater
kingdom. The realm was made of sparkling shells
and colorful coral.

The Sea King lived with his six daughters. Each
daughter could sing beautifully, but the youngest,
the littlest mermaid, had the most angelic voice
of them all.

Even though the little mermaid loved her family and their magical kingdom, she longed to turn fifteen, when she would be allowed to swim up to the water's surface for the first time.

"I want to see what life is like up there," she told her sisters, dreamily.

On her fifteenth birthday, she
swam to the surface. The first thing
she saw was a pretty fireworks display
lighting up the starry sky. She then
noticed a ship, and on board a
handsome man wearing a crown.
"He's a prince!" she said to herself.

Moments later, the wind picked up. Thick clouds filled the sky and the stars disappeared. The wind soon grew strong and bolts of lightning struck the water. The rain came down heavily and huge waves lashed the side of the ship.

Suddenly, the boat capsized and the prince was tossed into the churning sea.

The little mermaid swam quickly to save the prince. She held his head above the water until the storm passed and the sea became calm.

When morning broke, the prince's ship was nowhere to be seen, so she carried him to shore and laid him down softly on the sparkling sand.

The little mermaid
began singing to the
prince. Slowly, he opened
his eyes and smiled. Her voice
was the most beautiful sound he
had ever heard.

Just then, the little mermaid saw people
walking toward them. Scared they would see
her tail, she dove back into the water.

Back in the underwater kingdom, the little mermaid told her sisters about her chance meeting with the prince. "All I want is to be human so I can be with him!" she said.

"The Sea Witch can make your wish come true," said one of the sisters. "But, beware, she always wants something in return."

The little mermaid swam to the darkest depths of the ocean in search of the Sea Witch. When she arrived, the enchantress knew exactly why the little mermaid had come.

"Drink this potion," the Sea Witch cackled, "and it will turn you human. But you will NEVER be able to speak or sing again. Your voice will belong to me!"

"Secondly, if the prince hasn't asked you to marry him before sunset on his next birthday then you shall live with me forever!"

Without her voice, the little mermaid knew how difficult it would be to win the prince's heart, but she wanted to see him so much, she accepted the Sea Witch's offer.

The little mermaid drank the potion. At once her tail turned into legs and she was whisked back to the shore, where the prince found her.

Realizing she was lost and couldn't speak, the prince decided to help her. Soon they became good friends. One day he told her how he wished to marry the girl who had rescued him. "She had the most beautiful voice," he said.

Time passed quickly and the prince's birthday was almost upon them. The little mermaid longed to reveal to the prince who she really was, but without her voice she could neither speak nor sing. Gloom filled her heart every time she remembered the deal she had made with the Sea Witch.

On the morning of the prince's birthday, the little mermaid looked out longingly at the ocean, wishing her sisters were here to help her.

Suddenly, she spotted something in the water. She rubbed her eyes because she could not believe her wish had come true. Her sisters rose to the surface of the water to see her. "We're so glad we found you!" they hollered.

"We've defeated the Sea Witch!" said the little mermaid's eldest sister. "She's gone forever and we have rescued your voice."

She held out the glowing bottle that contained the little mermaid's voice. The little mermaid took the bottle, pulled the cork out, and drank from it right away.

"Thank you!" gasped the little mermaid. Her voice was back and she was delighted! She began to sing the most beautiful song.

The prince recognized the voice immediately. He turned around and realized that it belonged to his friend. He rushed toward her. "You," he gasped. "It was you who rescued me!"

The prince asked the little mermaid to marry him and she accepted right away.

Their wonderful wedding took place at the royal castle overlooking the sea.

As the waves lapped the shore, the little mermaid's sisters danced in the water in celebration. The little mermaid's dream had come true!

Cinderella

A long time ago there was an orhpan girl who lived with her terribly cruel stepmother and stepsisters. The family would make her do all the chores. Her stepsisters called her "Cinderella" because she was always covered in the ash and cinders from sleeping by their filthy fireplace.

One day, the king announced that there was to be a three-day feast for the prince. Every lady in the kingdom was invited to three balls at the palace. Cinderella's stepsisters were ecstatic!

"Comb our hair, Cinderella!" they ordered.

"Lace up our dresses, Cinderella!"

"Polish our shoes, Cinderella!"

Cinderella helped her sisters get ready for the
first ball, but she was incredibly sad. She begged
her stepmother to let her go, too.

"You can't possibly go to a ball looking like that!"
snapped her stepmother. "You have nothing but
rags to wear and shabby slippers on your feet."

After her stepsisters and mother had gone to the ball, Cinderella, alone in the house, began to sob.

Then, magically, her fairy godmother appeared.

The fairy godmother knew why Cinderella was upset. "Listen very carefully, my dear," she began, "and you shall go to the ball."

"Fetch me the biggest pumpkin you can find," said the fairy godmother.
So that's just what Cinderella did.

Then, with one simple flick of her magic wand, the fairy godmother transformed the lumpy orange pumpkin into the most beautiful golden carriage Cinderella had ever seen!

"Oh my!" she gasped, amazed.

Next, the fairy godmother turned two mice into stunning white horses to pull the carriage, a rat into a well-dressed coachman to drive the horses, and two lizards into fancy footmen.

Finally, with another flick of her wand, she turned Cinderella's dirty rags into a dazzling dress!

Cinderella was amazed. She had everything she needed to attend the grand ball.

"Now, you shall go to the ball," announced her fairy godmother. "But you must return home before midnight. At the stroke of midnight everything will turn back to how it was before."

The grand ball at the palace was exquisite. Cinderella was thrilled when the prince asked her for a dance.

They spent the whole night spinning and twirling across the magnificent marble dance floor. Cinderella's stepsisters and stepmother didn't even recognize her in her stunning ball gown.

Remembering her fairy godmother's warning, Cinderella made sure she left the ball in plenty of time before midnight.

When she arrived home and the clock struck midnight, her coach turned back into a pumpkin, horses into mice, coachman into a rat, footmen into lizards, and finally her dress into rags.

BONG!

On the night of the second ball, after her
stepmother and stepsisters had left for the palace,
Cinderella's fairy godmother appeared again.

"You shall go to the second ball!" she announced.
And with another wave of her wand she magically
transformed everything again. She turned Cinderella's
rags into a gorgeous, shimmering gown.

As soon as Cinderella arrived at the second ball, the prince whisked her off. The couple danced together for the rest of the evening.

They had so much fun, until Cinderella noticed the time on the clock. It was close to midnight!

"Oh my," she cried.

"What's the matter?" asked the prince.

"I must go," she replied.

"But why?"

Cinderella had no time to explain. So she said goodbye and left before the magic wore off.

On the night of the final ball, Cinderella's fairy godmother turned her rags into a dazzling white dress. Once again she reminded Cinderella to be home by midnight.

Cinderella had such a great time with the prince she forgot to look at the clock. Suddenly, it began to strike midnight.

BONG!

Cinderella raced down the palace stairs.

The stunned prince ran after Cinderella, but
she had already disappeared beyond the woods.
"She's left her shoe behind," he said, picking
up the glass slipper that had come off her foot. It
was specially made to fit a foot like none other.
"This slipper will help me find her," he said to
himself. "And then I will ask her to marry me."

The prince searched the realm for the mystery princess. One young woman after another tried on the glass slipper, but none could fit into it.

Finally, he arrived at Cinderella's house.

Try as they might, the stepsisters just could not squeeze their feet into the dainty glass slipper.

The prince then noticed the girl in dirty rags standing in corner of the room. He saw something familiar in her eyes.

"Please try on the slipper," he asked Cinderella, to the utter dismay of her stepsisters.

Cinderella came forward, sat down, and slowly slid her foot into the elegant glass slipper.

"It fits!" gasped the prince. He looked deep into Cinderella's beautiful eyes. "I can't believe it! It's you. I danced with you at the palace."

"Yes!" she cried. "It was me." Cinderella's stepsisters and stepmother looked horrified. And, when the prince asked Cinderella to marry him they fainted in shock!

Cinderella and the prince celebrated by having the prettiest wedding at the palace. There was delicious food, plenty of joy and laughter, and lots and lots of dancing . . . even after the clock struck midnight!

Beauty and
the Beast

A poor merchant had three daughters. The youngest, called Beauty, was the kindest of the three.

One day, when the merchant was leaving for work, he asked each daughter what gift they wanted him to bring back from his trip. While her sisters asked for expensive jewelry, Beauty asked only for a single rose.

On his way home,
the merchant was caught
in a frightful storm and
lost his way. Wet, cold, and
weary, he came across a castle
that looked warm inside. When
he knocked on the door there was no
answer. He realized the door was ajar
and stepped inside for shelter.

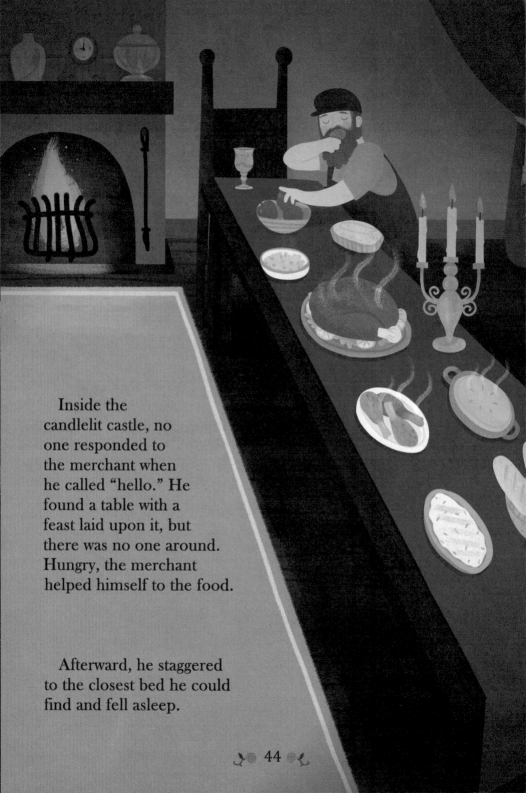

Inside the candlelit castle, no one responded to the merchant when he called "hello." He found a table with a feast laid upon it, but there was no one around. Hungry, the merchant helped himself to the food.

Afterward, he staggered to the closest bed he could find and fell asleep.

The next morning, the merchant explored the grounds of the castle and came across a delightful rose garden. He breathed in the sweet smelling flowers, which reminded him of the gift Beauty had asked for.

As he picked a rose for her, he heard a strange growling sound coming from behind him.

"How dare you pick my roses after I let you eat my food and stay in my castle!" boomed a terrifying creature. "Now I will punish you!"
    The merchant was petrified. He said sorry to the beast and begged not to be harmed.

"You may leave on one condition," said the Beast.
"You must return in thirty days' time, bringing with you
whomever first greets you when you get home. You will
leave that person to live with me forever."

The merchant agreed at once. He galloped off on
his horse. When he arrived home the first person
to spot him was his youngest daughter.

Beauty ran toward him, waving her arms in excitement. She had been eagerly awaiting his return and was beaming with joy.

"Father!" she gasped, delighted to see him. "You're back!"

Once indoors, Beauty noticed the sad look on her father's face.

"What's wrong, father?" she asked.

The merchant told his daughter about his encounter with the Beast and the promise he had been forced to make.

"But I will not take you to him," he added.

"You must keep your promise," Beauty insisted. "It's only right that you do."

So, as promised, thirty days later, the merchant returned to the Beast's castle with Beauty.

"Welcome!" bellowed the Beast in his booming voice.

"Hello," whispered Beauty, glancing back at her father nervously.

"Now you must go," the Beast told the merchant. After her father left, Beauty felt alone and afraid.

Over time, Beauty feared the
Beast less and less. She soon learned
how kind and generous he was.
They spent lots of time taking walks
together, reading and talking. And
the more time they spent together,
the more they fell in love.

One day, Beauty looked into the
Beast's magical mirror. She saw her
father sick in bed. Although the
Beast was worried Beauty might
not return if she left to see her
father, he let her leave the castle.
"Put this ring on your finger
when you wish to return," he said.

Beauty nursed her father back to health. She decided to stay with him until he was fully well again, but had a horrible dream one night that the Beast was dying without her. She woke up and immediately put his ring on her finger.

In the morning, Beauty woke up to find she was back in the castle. The Beast was lying on the ground, just like in her dream. *Was he dying?* She rushed over to help him.

"Oh please don't die, please. I love you so much . . ." she cried.

The Beast opened his eyes to see that his beloved had returned.

Suddenly, the Beast magically transformed into a prince! He picked himself up and stood in front of Beauty.

"I love you, too, Beauty," he said, the growl no longer in his voice. "More than anyone in this world." Beauty was stunned! "You're a prince?" she gasped.

The prince explained that long ago a wicked fairy had cast a spell on him that turned him into a frightful beast.

"The only thing that could break the curse was finding someone who truly loved me," said the prince, "and that person is you, Beauty."

The prince saw the magic ring on Beauty's finger. "You still have the ring I gave you," he rejoiced. "Will you marry me?"

"Oh yes!" Beauty replied, for she loved him dearly.

The wedding was held in the pretty rose garden at the prince's castle. Beauty could not have been happier. Her father was well again and gave her away to the person she had fallen in love with.

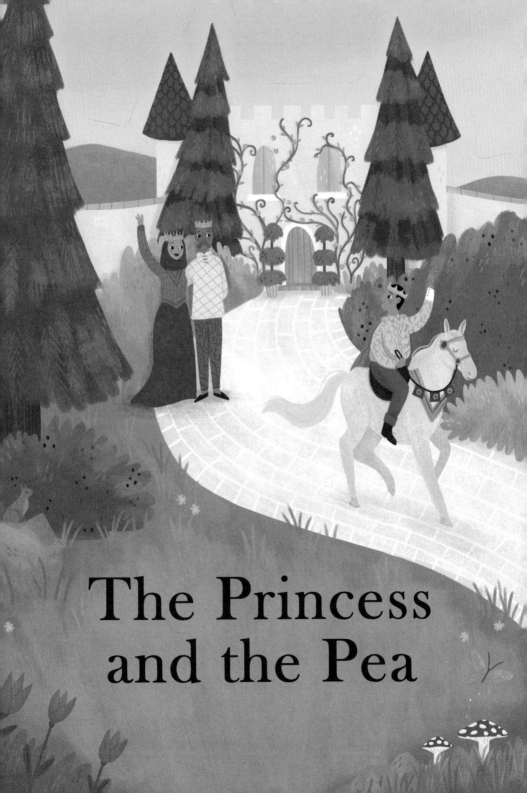

The Princess
and the Pea

There was once a prince who wished to marry a princess. But only a real princess would do, so he traveled all across the realm in search of his perfect bride.

On his search he found plenty
of young maidens who claimed to
be princesses, but he felt none were
right for him.

Some were unkind or spoke with a rude
voice, while others had bad table manners or
a laugh that made them sound like a hyena!

After many months the prince finally gave up his search and returned home.

"What happened?" the queen asked as the prince shuffled into the palace with a glum look on his face.

"There isn't a single princess in the realm who is right for me!" he replied.

The king and queen knew how eager their son was to find a wife who was gentle and delicate, with a soft-hearted soul worthy of a true princess.

"Don't despair, my son," consoled the queen. "When the time is right you will find your perfect princess."

One evening, a terrible storm raged
outside with thunder, lightning, and
heavy rain. In the middle of it all there
was a knock on the door of the castle.

"Who could that be?" the
king mumbled to himself as he
went to answer the door.

When the king opened the door, he saw standing before him a young lady. She was wet from head to toe and her teeth were chattering from the cold.

"My goodness!" said the king.
"You had better come inside."

Hearing the king's voice, the queen came out of their chamber to see what was going on.

"Oh my," she said at the sight of the sopping wet young lady. "What were you doing outside during a storm?"

Although the young lady was trembling
from the cold, she managed to greet the
queen with a curtsey.

"I am sorry for intruding at this late hour, your majesty,"
she said meekly. "I lost my way and got caught in the storm.
Please may I take shelter here until the storm passes?"

Both the king and queen were taken aback by how politely the young girl spoke. They also noticed that she was dressed in fine clothes.

"Who are you?" they asked.
"I am a princess."
"Is that so?" said the queen.

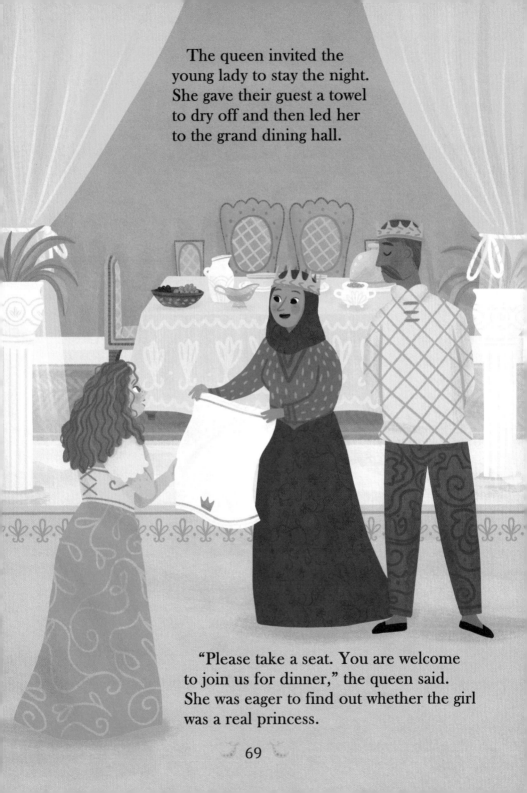

The queen invited the
young lady to stay the night.
She gave their guest a towel
to dry off and then led her
to the grand dining hall.

"Please take a seat. You are welcome
to join us for dinner," the queen said.
She was eager to find out whether the girl
was a real princess.

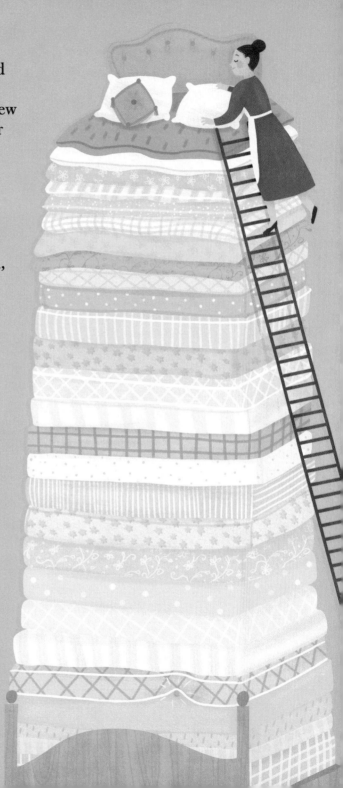

The queen left the dining room and headed to the royal guest room. She knew just how to test their guest and find out whether she was telling the truth.

In the guest room, the queen stripped back the sheets and put a pea on the bed. She made the chambermaid stack twenty mattresses on top and pile another twenty goose-feather quilts over the mattresses. The princess was to spend the night on top of all these.

The next morning, the queen
asked the girl how she slept.
"You can speak the truth,"
the queen said, encouragingly.

"I barely closed my eyes
all night," the girl replied.
"Who knows what was
pressing against my back.
I just couldn't sleep!"

The queen beamed with joy. She went to tell the king the good news right away. Meanwhile, the prince fell in love with their guest the moment he laid eyes on her.

"Nobody but a real princess could have
such delicate skin that she felt the pea through
twenty mattresses and twenty feather quilts!"
the queen told the king. The couple celebrated
because they knew their son's search was over.

The king and queen watched as the prince got down on one knee.

He took the princess's hand and asked her if she would marry him.

"Yes!" she replied.

A grand royal wedding took place at the castle.

The subjects gathered in the courtyard to see their prince marry a true princess. They cheered once the couple were married and celebrated well into the night.

The pea was placed in the royal museum, where it is on display for the whole world to see and learn how it helped the queen find the perfect princess for her son.

Thumbelina

An old woman lived alone in a cottage on a hill. She spent her days looking after her flowers. One day, a witch came along and gave the old woman a special seed. "Plant this, water it daily, and you shall be rewarded."

The old woman obeyed the witch's instructions. A few days later a beautiful pink flower sprouted up from the earth. After a week the flower blossomed, revealing a small girl with long dark hair.

The girl was no larger than a thumb so the
old woman named her Thumbelina.
    She raised Thumbelina as her own daughter.

Thumbelina had the most beautiful
singing voice and each night she would
sing the old woman to sleep.

One summer evening, a large toad hopped up to the window after hearing Thumbelina's lovely voice. Once Thumbelina had fallen asleep, the toad crept in through the window.

"Oh my! She will make the perfect wife for my son!" the toad exclaimed. She grabbed Thumbelina and carried her off to the nearby river.

"Look at the lovely bride I've found you!" the toad said to her son. She placed Thumbelina on the smallest lily pad.

Thumbelina woke up just as mother toad and son had gone to sleep. Thumbelina felt homesick and began to cry.

Two orange fish heard Thumbelina weeping.
They swam over to Thumbelina's lily pad, chewed
at the stalk and set her free.

"Thank you so much," Thumbelina exclaimed, as she
began floating away downstream. But she ended up on a
riverbank even farther away from her dear old mother.

Thumbelina felt sad and lonely at first, but soon became friends with the butterflies, dragonflies, and bumblebees.

In the winter, she found shelter in a tunnel where a blind mole lived. The mole heard Thumbelina's singing and fell in love with her immediately.

"You can stay with me," he said.

One day, Thumbelina noticed a bird lying in the tunnel. "What is this beautiful creature?" she asked.

"It's just a lazy bird!" answered the mole. "Don't give it any attention," he added. He then took Thumbelina's hand and led her away.

Later on, Thumbelina returned to check on the bird and realized that it was weak and unwell. She spent the winter nursing it back to health, singing to it every night.

When spring came, the bird was healthy again and ready to leave for the summer.

"Join me, Thumbelina," he said. "We'll be flying around all day in the warm sunshine."

Thumbelina wanted to go but could not to leave the mole on his own. She sadly waved goodbye to the bird as it soared into the sky.

In the fall, the blind mole
asked Thumbelina to marry him.

"Please may I think about it?"
she replied, for she didn't want to
hurt the mole's feelings.

Afterward, Thumbelina
felt sad at the thought of
spending the rest of her
days with the mole in a
dark, cold place.

One morning, Thumbelina
gazed up at the late fall sunshine
and spotted the bird she had
rescued. The bird flew down
and perched beside her.

"I'm flying to the land of summer," said the bird.
"Why don't you come with me, Thumbelina?"

This time Thumbelina didn't think twice. She climbed onto the bird's back and they flew off. After traveling for days the bird landed on a flowery meadow and left Thumbelina on a large pink flower.

All of a sudden, a young man, who was the same size as Thumbelina, appeared from behind a large pink petal. He claimed to be the prince of the kingdom.

After spending many happy weeks with Thumbelina,
the prince placed his brilliant crown upon Thumbelina's
head and asked her to be his bride.

Years later, the bird flew
past the old woman's cottage
singing Thumbelina's song.
The old woman recognized
the song instantly.

He was kinder than the mole and made Thumbelina
feel cherished. So she happily said "Yes!"

Upon hearing the song, the old
woman was no longer sad, for she
knew that Thumbelina was safe and
living happily in a faraway land.

Main Characters

The Little Mermaid

Prince

Queen

Princess

Fairy

Cinderella

Prince

Father

Beauty

Beast

Thumbelina